HATE

AN'OTHER' WAY TO LOVE

OMKAR PALIKA

Made with ♥ on the Notion Press Platform
www.notionpress.com

To all my dear friends and users,

This book is dedicated to each and every one of you who has supported and encouraged me throughout my journey. Your enthusiasm and curiosity have inspired me to explore new ideas and topics, and to push myself beyond my limits.

Thank you for being a part of this experience, and for helping me grow into the best version of myself. I hope that this book has brought you joy, entertainment, and perhaps even a new perspective on love, relationships, and life.

With love and gratitude,

~ Omkar Palika ~

~ Hani ~

Contents

Preface

Love is a beautiful, yet unpredictable journey. It takes us to unexpected places and makes us feel things we never thought possible. Sometimes it comes when we least expect it, and other times, it's been there all along, waiting for us to open our hearts to it.

This is a story about two people, Riya and Dhruv, whose paths cross in a way that changes both of their lives forever. They were brought together by fate, and their love story is a testament to the power of destiny.

But their journey is not an easy one. It's filled with challenges, obstacles, and unexpected twists that test their love and their commitment to each other. Riya and Dhruv's love is not perfect, but it is real, and it's worth fighting for.

This is a story about second chances, forgiveness, and the unbreakable bond between two people who are meant to be together. It's about learning to let go of the past and embracing the present, even when it's not what we expected.

So come along for the ride and join Riya and Dhruv on their journey of love, loss, and redemption.

Foreword

Welcome to the world of Riya and Dhruv, a couple who found love in unexpected circumstances. Their journey together is one filled with love, challenges, and personal growth. This book is a tale of how two people from different walks of life come together, and the obstacles they face along the way. It is a story about family, forgiveness, and the power of love.

As you read through the pages of this book, you will experience the ups and downs of Riya and Dhruv's relationship. You will see the struggles they face as they try to navigate through life's surprises and curveballs. But through it all, their love remains steadfast and unbreakable.

This book is for anyone who has ever loved, lost, and loved again. It is for those who have been through the ups and downs of a relationship and come out stronger on the other side. It is a story of hope and the power of perseverance.

So sit back, relax, and let Riya and Dhruv's story take you on a journey of love and self-discovery. Enjoy the ride!

Acknowledgements

I would like to express my deep gratitude to all the people who have supported me throughout this journey. Your encouragement and feedback have been invaluable, and I couldn't have done this without you. Thank you.

~Hani

I would like to express my sincere thanks to all the individuals who have supported and inspired me throughout my writing journey. Your encouragement and feedback have been invaluable.

~Omkar Palika

"Finally, I want to thank the readers. Your interest in this story and willingness to take a chance on a new author is a gift beyond measure. Thank you for coming on this journey with me."

Prologue

As the sun slowly rises over the city, Riya sits at her kitchen table with a cup of coffee in her hand, lost in thought. She can't believe how much her life has changed in just a few short weeks.

She thinks back to the day when she met Dhruv, the man who would turn her world upside down. At the time, she had no idea how much he would come to mean to her and how their lives would become intertwined.

But that was just the beginning. What Riya didn't know at the time was that the universe had more in store for her. More twists and turns, more unexpected surprises that would push her to her limits and test her love for Dhruv in ways she could never have imagined.

As Riya takes another sip of her coffee, she braces herself for the journey ahead. She knows that whatever comes next, she will face it with determination and the unwavering belief that love can conquer all.

CHAPTER ONE

The Rivalry Begin

Riya and Dhruv first met on the debate team in high school. Both of them were passionate about debating and winning. They were both top debaters and often found themselves facing off against each other. From the very beginning, Riya and Dhruv did not get along. They were both highly competitive, and their rivalry was fierce. They would often argue and bicker with each other during debates, and their exchanges would become more heated as the competition intensified. Riya found Dhruv to be arrogant and overconfident, always boasting about his skills as a debater. She thought that he was too full of himself and did not take kindly to his attitude. On the other hand, Dhruv found Riya to be too serious and uptight. He thought that she was too focused on winning and didn't know how to have fun. He would often tease her and make sarcastic comments, which would only serve to irritate her even more.

Their mutual animosity continued throughout their high school years. They would often compete against each other in various other activities such as science fairs and essay competitions, always trying to one-up each other.

Even when they were not competing against each other, they would still find ways to antagonize each other. Their rivalry became something of a legend in their school. Other students would often take sides and place bets on who would win in a face-off between Riya and Dhruv. Riya and Dhruv's rivalry had become so intense that they were known throughout the school as the ***"Debate Rivals"***. Despite their mutual dislike for each other, there was an underlying attraction between them. They both admired each other's intelligence and debating skills, even if they wouldn't admit it. They both felt a spark of chemistry when they were near each other, but they were too stubborn to act on it.

Riya and Dhruv had always been competitive, ever since their high school debate team days. They were both highly ambitious and driven, which made them natural rivals in both their personal and professional lives. Their rivalry had only intensified over the years, as they had both gone on to successful careers in the same field. They were constantly trying to one-up each other, whether it was with the latest project or the biggest client. Their latest encounter, at a conference in the next city over, was no different. As soon as they saw each other, they bristled with the same old tension and animosity.

But this time, things were about to take a turn...

CHAPTER TWO

Forced Together

As the conference drew to a close, the snow started to fall heavily outside. Riya and Dhruv realized too late that they had no way to get back to their hotel, which was a few hours away, and no one was willing to drive in the treacherous conditions. The only option left was to find a place to stay in the small town nearby. They set out into the snow-covered streets, determined to find a warm bed for the night. After trying every hotel in town with no success, they ended up at a small diner on the outskirts of town.

The owner of the diner offered them a room above the diner to stay in for the night. Riya and Dhruv reluctantly agreed to share the small room, both determined to ignore each other as much as possible. But as the night wore on and the storm raged outside, they found themselves drawn to each other, seeking warmth and comfort in their shared misery.

As they talked and laughed, they realized that they might have misjudged each other all these years.

Underneath all the competitiveness and rivalry, there was a connection between them that they had never acknowledged before. And as they finally fell asleep, wrapped up in each other's arms, they both wondered if this might be the start of something more.

CHAPTER THREE

BREAKING THE ICE

The next morning, Riya and Dhruv woke up in each other's arms, feeling rested and comfortable. They looked at each other with surprise, not quite sure what to make of their newfound closeness. They quickly got dressed and headed down to the diner for breakfast. As they ate, they chatted about their plans for the day and their predicament of being stuck in the small town. The owner of the diner overheard their conversation and offered to take them on a tour of the town. He pointed out local landmarks and interesting spots, including a beautiful park with a frozen lake. Riya and Dhruv were hesitant at first, but they decided to take the tour and make the most of their unexpected stay.

As they walked through the snow-covered streets, they started to see each other in a new light. Riya noticed how Dhruv's eyes lit up when he talked about his passion for his work, and Dhruv was impressed by Riya's dedication to her own career. They found that they had more in common than they thought and started to genuinely enjoy each other's company. As they reached the park, they decided to try their luck at ice skating on the frozen lake. It was a beautiful day and the sun was shining, making the snow sparkle like diamonds. They stumbled and fell, laughing at each other's lack of grace, but it only made them feel closer. As they held hands and skated together, they realized that they had fallen in love with each other.

After a few hours of skating and enjoying the winter wonderland, they made their way back to the diner for lunch. They sat across from each other, smiling and flirting, knowing that something had changed between them.

As they finished their meal, Dhruv couldn't help but lean in and kiss Riya on the cheek. Riya blushed and looked down, but inside she felt a sense of excitement and joy that she had never experienced before. It was clear that their competitive rivalry had turned into something much deeper, and they both knew that they were falling in love with each other. As they looked into each other's eyes, they knew that they wanted to take a chance on a real relationship, no matter the challenges that lay ahead.

CHAPTER FOUR

A New Perspective

As they talked, Riya and Dhruv began to see each other in a new light. They discovered that they had more in common than they had realized, and they found themselves enjoying each other's company more than they ever thought possible. After lunch, Riya and Dhruv continued their explorations of the small town. They stumbled upon an art museum and decided to go in and take a look. As they wandered through the exhibits, they shared their thoughts and opinions on the artwork. They were surprised to find that they had similar tastes and perspectives, and they found themselves appreciating the art more because they were experiencing it together.

As they left the museum and walked back to their lodging, Riya and Dhruv felt a newfound sense of closeness between them. They were enjoying each other's company more and more, and they felt an undeniable attraction growing.

But despite their feelings, neither of them was quite ready to take the next step. They were hesitant to risk the newfound friendship they had developed and uncertain about what starting a relationship might mean for them. As they reached their lodging, they exchanged a lingering glance and a small smile. It was a curious moment, full of unspoken feelings and desires, but they both knew that they needed more time to sort out their emotions before taking any further action. With a curious sense of anticipation, they said their greetings, wondering what the future might hold for them.

CHAPTER FIVE

THE FIRST KISS

Riya lay in bed that night, staring up at the ceiling and thinking about Dhruv. She couldn't stop thinking about the way he had looked at her that day, or the way his hand had brushed hers as they had walked back to their lodging.

As she drifted off to sleep, she realized that she was falling in love with him. It was a terrifying and exhilarating feeling, and she didn't know what to do about it.

The next morning, Riya woke up early and decided to take a walk by herself. As she walked through the snowy landscape, she tried to sort out her emotions and figure out what she wanted.

Suddenly, she heard footsteps behind her, and she turned around to see Dhruv approaching.

"Good morning," he said, smiling at her. *"Mind if I join you?"*

Riya smiled back and nodded, and the two of them walked together in comfortable silence for a few minutes.

Despite the intensity of their feelings for each other, both Riya and Dhruv couldn't help but feel a sense of uncertainty and hesitation about starting a relationship.

For Riya, it was the fear of getting hurt again. She had been in a few relationships before, but they had all ended in heartbreak. She was afraid that if she allowed herself to fall too deeply in love with Dhruv, he would eventually leave her too.

Dhruv, on the other hand, was hesitant because he had just gotten out of a long-term relationship. He wasn't sure if he was ready to jump into something new so soon, and he didn't want to hurt Riya by getting involved with her if he wasn't emotionally available.

Despite the uncertainty and hesitation, they couldn't deny the powerful attraction they felt for each other. They found themselves constantly drawn together, unable to resist the pull of their mutual desire.

Finally, Dhruv broke the silence. *"Riya, I know we've only known each other for a short time, but I feel like we have a connection. I don't want to rush into anything, but I have to be honest with you: I think I'm falling in love with you."*

Riya's heart skipped a beat. *"I feel the same way,"* she said softly.

Without another word, Dhruv leaned in and kissed her. It was a gentle, tentative kiss at first, but soon it deepened as they both gave in to their feelings for each other.

As they pulled away, they looked at each other with wonder and disbelief. They had been forced together, had started off hating each other, and had somehow ended up falling in love.

"I don't know what the future holds," Dhruv said, *"but I know that I want to be with you. Will you take a chance on me?"*

Riya smiled and took his hand. *"Yes,"* she said. *"I will."*

They knew that they were embarking on a new and uncertain journey together. But they also knew that they had each other, and that was enough to face whatever challenges lay ahead.

CHAPTER SIX

Working Through Differences

Riya and Dhruv returned from their trip feeling elated and excited about their new relationship. But as they settled back into their everyday lives, they soon realized that being together wasn't going to be easy.

Both of them were highly competitive individuals, used to being in control and getting their way. This often led to disagreements and arguments, as they each struggled to assert their own preferences and opinions.

Riya and Dhruv quickly realized that if they were going to make their relationship work, they needed to learn how to work through their differences. They started by talking openly and honestly with each other, listening to each other's perspectives and trying to find common ground.

They also learned the importance of compromise. Sometimes, one of them would have to give in to the other's wishes, even if it wasn't what they wanted. This wasn't always easy, but they both knew that it was necessary if they were going to build a strong and healthy relationship.

As they worked through their differences, they also began to learn more about each other. They discovered new things they had in common, and learned to appreciate each other's unique strengths and quirks.

Slowly but surely, Riya and Dhruv started to build a foundation of trust and understanding. They learned that their relationship wasn't always going to be easy, but they were committed to working through their challenges together.

Through it all, they held on to the memories of their trip to the snowy cabin, where they had first fallen in love. They knew that if they could make it through that difficult and uncertain time, they could make it through anything.

As their relationship grew stronger, Riya and Dhruv also made a conscious effort to support each other's individual goals and dreams. They encouraged each other to pursue their passions, even if it meant spending time apart.

This wasn't always easy, especially for two people who had grown accustomed to being together all the time. But they recognized the importance of maintaining their own identities and supporting each other's growth.

Riya and Dhruv also started to create new memories and traditions together, building a life that was uniquely theirs. They took weekend trips to nearby towns, tried new restaurants, and explored new hobbies.

Through it all, they knew that their relationship wasn't perfect. There were still moments of tension and frustration, but they had learned how to work through their differences in a constructive way.

They also knew that they couldn't predict the future, and that there were bound to be more challenges and obstacles to overcome. But as long as they had each other, they were confident that they could face anything together.

CHAPTER SEVEN

CONFLICTS AND COMPLICATIONS

Riya and Dhruv had built a strong and loving relationship, but soon they faced external challenges that tested their commitment to each other.

Dhruv's job became more demanding, leaving him with less time to spend with Riya. This led to feelings of loneliness and isolation, as Riya struggled to adjust to Dhruv's new schedule.

In addition to external challenges, personal issues and past traumas also resurfaced, putting a strain on their relationship. Riya's anxiety and depression began to take a toll on her mental health, while Dhruv struggled with trust issues from past relationships.

As they faced these challenges, Riya and Dhruv tried their best to support each other. They listened and provided comfort, offering a shoulder to lean on when the other needed it most.

But they also realized that they needed to take care of themselves, and sought professional help to address their personal issues.

Despite their efforts, there were moments of frustration and tension in their relationship. They struggled to communicate effectively, often falling into old patterns of defensiveness and blame. It seemed as though their relationship was slowly unraveling.

But as they confronted their personal issues and worked through their communication struggles, they started to find a new appreciation for each other. They realized that they had been taking each other for granted, and that they needed to actively work to keep their relationship strong.

As they emerged from these conflicts and complications, Riya and Dhruv were more committed than ever to each other. They knew that their love was worth fighting for, and that they could weather any storm as long as they faced it together.

CHAPTER EIGHT

THE BIG GESTURE

Riya and Dhruv had been through their share of challenges, but their love for each other only grew stronger. And one day, one of them decided to make a grand gesture to show their commitment to the relationship.

Riya had been thinking about it for a while, and finally decided to surprise Dhruv with a romantic evening. She planned out every detail, from the candlelit dinner to the music playlist, all with the aim of showing Dhruv just how much she loved him.

As Dhruv walked in, he was immediately struck by the scene before him. The table was set with Riya's finest dishes, and the room was filled with the soft glow of candlelight. He could hear the strains of their favorite love songs playing in the background, and he knew that this was Riya's way of telling him how much he meant to her.

Over dinner, Riya and Dhruv talked about their future together, and reaffirmed their commitment to each other. They talked about the challenges they had faced, and how much they had learned about themselves and each other through it all.

As the night wore on, Riya and Dhruv danced to their favorite songs, and shared their hopes and dreams for the future. They both knew that their love was worth fighting for, and they were determined to make their relationship work, no matter what challenges lay ahead.

As the evening drew to a close, Riya and Dhruv shared a kiss, sealing their commitment to each other. They both knew that there would still be ups and downs, but they were more confident than ever that they could weather any storm as long as they faced it together.

CHAPTER NINE

Overcoming Obstacles

Riya and Dhruv had weathered many storms, but their love for each other only grew stronger. They knew that they could overcome any obstacle as long as they faced it together.

As they navigated the ups and downs of their relationship, Riya and Dhruv encountered new challenges that tested their commitment to each other. External obstacles, such as work stress and family issues, threatened to pull them apart. But they were determined to fight for their love and their relationship.

Riya and Dhruv also faced internal obstacles, as their own fears and insecurities sometimes got in the way of their happiness. But they learned to trust and support each other through the tough times, and this only made their love stronger.

They worked together to find solutions to their problems, and learned to communicate openly and honestly with each other. They made compromises and sacrifices when necessary, knowing that their love was worth it.

As they overcame each obstacle, Riya and Dhruv's love deepened and grew. They knew that they were stronger together than they could ever be apart.

Finally, after much hard work and dedication, Riya and Dhruv emerged from their trials as a stronger, more resilient couple. They knew that their love was something special, and they were grateful for the obstacles they had faced, as they had only made them appreciate each other more.

As they looked back on their journey together, they knew that they were ready for whatever the future held. They were confident in their love and in each other, and they knew that they would face whatever challenges came their way, together.

CHAPTER TEN

Happily Ever After...Or Is It?

After months of ups and downs, Riya and Dhruv finally found themselves in a place of peace and contentment. They had worked through their conflicts and overcome their obstacles, and their love had only grown stronger as a result.

As they sat together, looking out at the sunset, Riya knew that Dhruv was the one she wanted to spend the rest of her life with. And as if he could read her mind, Dhruv reached into his pocket and pulled out a small velvet box.

Riya's heart skipped a beat as he got down on one knee and opened the box to reveal a sparkling diamond ring. *"Riya, will you marry me?"* he asked.

Tears streaming down her face, Riya said yes, knowing that this was the start of their forever.

The months that followed were filled with wedding planning, family gatherings, and the excitement of starting a new life together. Riya and Dhruv knew that there would still be challenges ahead, but they were ready to face them together.

As they exchanged their vows on a beautiful summer day, surrounded by their loved ones, Riya and Dhruv knew that their love story had come full circle. They had overcome their differences and worked through their struggles, and now they were ready to start a new chapter in their lives as husband and wife.

With a renewed sense of commitment and a lifetime of love ahead of them, Riya and Dhruv knew that they would always be each other's rock. And as they danced together under the stars, they knew that they had found their happily ever after.

As the night wore on, and the wedding guests started to leave, Riya and Dhruv found themselves alone. It was then that Dhruv turned to Riya with a serious expression.

"Riya, there's something I need to tell you," he said, his voice trembling slightly.

Riya's heart raced as she waited for him to speak.

"I just found out that I have a daughter," he said, his eyes filling with tears.

Riya was shocked and didn't know what to say. Dhruv had never mentioned anything about having a child before.

"I didn't know about her until recently, but I want to be a part of her life," he continued.

Riya listened as Dhruv explained the complicated circumstances that had led to his daughter's existence. She could see the pain and uncertainty in his eyes, and knew that they would have to work through this new challenge together.

And with that revelation, Riya and Dhruv's perfect wedding day ended with a twist that would lead them down a new path in the next book of their love story.

To Be Continued....!

"If you enjoyed reading this book, please consider leaving a review. Your feedback is greatly appreciated and will help others discover this book."

9 798889 865377

Printed by Libri Plureos GmbH in Hamburg, Germany